Based on the true story of a fearless ninja
and her network of female spies

SHADOW
WARRIOR

BY TANYA LLOYD KYI
ILLUSTRATIONS BY CELIA KRAMPIEN

annick press
toronto + berkeley

Designed by Bambi Edlund
Text review by Shoko Nagai and Faron Cosco

Annick Press Ltd.

We acknowledge the support of the Canada Council for the Arts and the Ontario Arts Council, and the participation of the Government of Canada/la participation du gouvernement du Canada for our publishing activities.

Library and Archives Canada Cataloging in Publication

Kyi, Tanya Lloyd, 1973–, author
        Shadow warrior / Tanya Lloyd Kyi ; illustrations by Celia Krampien.

Includes bibliographical references.
Issued in print and electronic formats.
ISBN 978-1-55451-966-8 (hardcover).—ISBN 978-1-55451-965-1 (softcover).—ISBN 978-1-55451-967-5 (HTML).—ISBN 978-1-55451-968-2 (PDF)

        I. Krampien, Celia, illustrator   II. Title.

PS8571.Y52S53 2017   jC813'.6   C2017-901551-6
                                                      C2017-901552-4

Published in the U.S.A. by Annick Press (U.S.) Ltd.
Distributed in Canada by University of Toronto Press.
Distributed in the U.S.A. by Publishers Group West.

Printed in China

annickpress.com
tanyalloydkyi.com
celiakrampien.com

Also available in e-book format. Please visit www.annickpress.com/ebooks.html for more details. Or scan

SHADOW WARRIOR

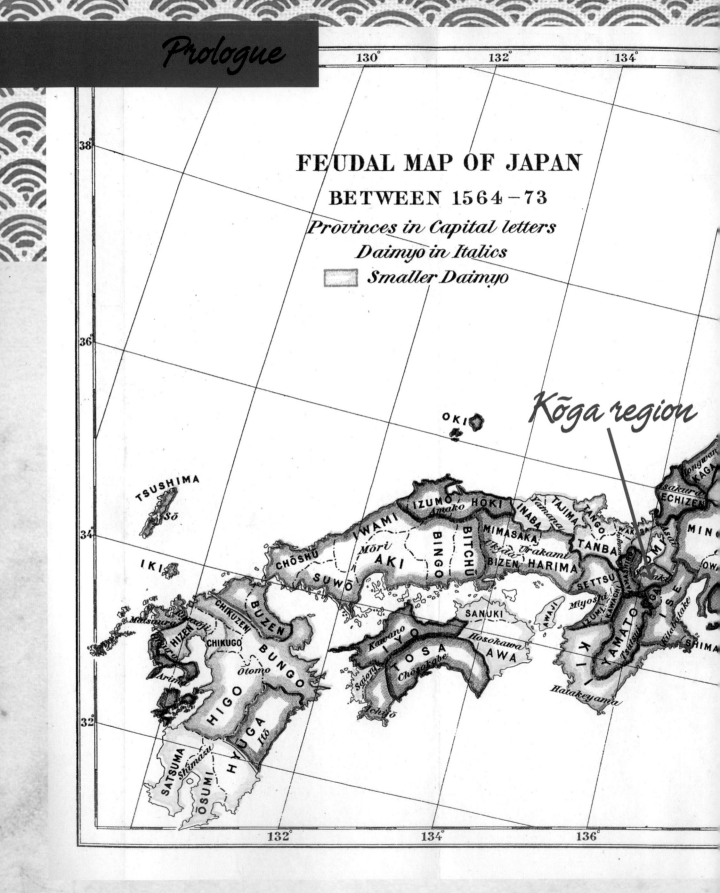

FEUDAL MAP OF JAPAN

BETWEEN 1564 – 73

Provinces in Capital letters
Daimyo in Italics
Smaller Daimyo

Kōga region

In the 1500s, Japan was battered by war.

The country was broken into small states, ruled over by hundreds of warlords called daimyos. Each had his own castle and army of samurai warriors. Daimyos fought constant, brutal battles for power and land, leaving children orphaned and towns destroyed.

In the rugged Kōga region, a few small villages formed a quiet refuge from war. Tucked between treacherous mountain passes, the area was difficult for enemy armies to reach. But Kōga also had a secret weapon:

ninjas.

Mochizuki Chiyome was determined to be one of them.

CHIYOME DANGLED upside down from the cliff's edge. The blood rushed to her head, and the pounding in her ears drowned out the calls of forest birds. The breeze, which had seemed so mild a moment ago, now threatened to tear her from the rock.

Her training partner adjusted his grip on her ankles, giving them a tiny tug. Chiyome held back a scream. The rocks at the base of the cliff were jagged and seemed heart-stoppingly far below. If she fell …

Be patient.

Conquer fear.

Sensei's words from that morning echoed in her head.

She glimpsed her instructor on the cliff's edge above, watching her silently. The other students, all boys, clustered nearby. Most had already completed this particular challenge.

She forced herself to take long, slow breaths as their voices drifted down to her.

"She'll give up soon."

"Maybe. But you know who her great-grandfather was, right?"

"Who?"

"Mochizuki Izumo-no-kami."

A murmur ran through the group at the sound of his name. He'd been one of Kōga's best fighters.

Chiyome felt her legs trembling. *Be patient. Conquer fear*, she repeated to herself. She remembered Sensei's lessons about practicing *zanshin*: calm awareness. She tried to clear her mind, ignoring the boys and focusing only on the rhythm of her breath and the cold wind on her face.

For just a whisper of time the fear seemed to float away from her body before she heard Sensei speak: "Bring her up."

Once again Chiyome began to shiver. Her partner gripped her legs tighter as another boy reached down for her hand, and together they hauled her up over the edge, the rough granite scraping her elbows and knees. She sprawled on the ground, gasping for air, and glanced at her partner. He looked as shaken as she felt. Then she forced herself upright and bowed to Sensei, who nodded his approval.

"Next," Sensei called, and a boy to her right stepped unsteadily forward.

Chiyome leaned against a tree trunk. Another ninja test, and she had survived. Not only survived, but gained a rare nod from her teacher. Though she kept her face carefully smooth, she was beaming inside.

Once, her great-grandfather had helped establish Kōga's ninja traditions. Now, Chiyome would carry on his legacy. She'd serve as one of the guards and lookouts who ranged through the nearby mountains, protecting the local villages. Or she'd seek her fortune working for a faraway daimyo.

First, she needed to learn everything Sensei could teach: how to scale castle walls, how to make waterproof torches, and how to count the sleeping bodies in a darkened room. She'd practice disguising herself in the light and listening from the shadows.

Today's tests had just begun. As the last boy pulled his partner up over the edge, Sensei ordered them all to their feet. They'd be hiking down the mountain, he explained, and practicing their rock climbing once they reached the bottom.

Chiyome hurried after him along the ridge, ignoring the drops on either side and refusing to think of the challenge still to come.

Zanshin. Be patient. Conquer fear.

CHIYOME PICKED HER WAY OVER ROOTS AND FALLEN TREES. For three days, she'd foraged for edible plants and followed wildlife trails through the woods. She'd sparked her own fires and slept on the embers at night to keep herself warm. But now, she was exhausted. Her legs felt as thin and limp as pickled vegetables. And these trees … there was still no sign of light between them. The forest was starting to blur into endless brown and green. She struggled to keep herself pointed in the same direction.

And then, finally, a hill she recognized. A thinning of tree trunks, and a glimpse of sun between them. She forced herself onward.

Chiyome finally emerged, battered and bruised, at the forest's edge.

Sensei remained stone-faced as she approached. But after a moment, she caught a glint in her teacher's eye.

"An interesting disguise for a ninja," he said. "Are you covered in dirt to match the trees?"

She barely heard his teasing. *A ninja!* She repeated it to herself as she ran home. He'd called her a ninja. And her challenge in the forest had marked the end of her training. She could do anything now. She could seek work, she could travel …

As she neared her house, she saw visitors leaving. They wore formal clothing with swords at their hips. She spotted a round *mon*, or crest, on one of the men, but she couldn't see it closely enough to spot the family pattern before they stalked away.

"Who were those men?" she asked her parents, both still standing in the doorway.

"Visitors from Kōfu," her father replied.

Chiyome's eyes widened. Hours to the northeast, Kōfu was the home of Takeda Shingen, one of the most powerful daimyos in all of Japan. People called him The Tiger because he was so ruthless and hungry for power.

"You'll be going there next week," Chiyome's father continued.

"To … to be a ninja?" she asked.

He laughed drily. "No. To be married, to Takeda Shingen's nephew. A samurai," he said.

"A good match," her mother added.

Chiyome half-listened as her parents discussed her escort for the road, and the honor of associating their family with that of Takeda Shingen. "This could be another layer of protection for Kōga," her father said.

Chiyome's head was spinning. An hour ago, she'd been dreaming of work as a spy and a warrior; now she was about to be married. She felt as if an earthquake was shaking her whole life. But for years, Sensei had taught her about duty, to her family and to her village. She struggled for acceptance. Was it possible she was never supposed to be a ninja? Maybe this marriage was her destiny.

TAKEDA SHINGEN STOOD in the largest room of his manor house, his relatives gathered on all sides to watch the wedding ceremony. He gazed with satisfaction at his nephew, the groom. Mochizuki Moritoki was a strong fighter with a keen mind. He'd be useful in upcoming battles.

And his new wife, standing even now before the Shinto priest … she was an interesting one.

He smothered a smile as the girl sipped the ritual sake and coughed. She was probably overwhelmed by the riches of his home and the number of new family members around her, but if so, she hid it well. Ninja training, he'd heard.

Ninjas. He'd love to turn them loose on Uesugi Kenshin. That daimyo was a constant problem. Even now, he was probably sitting within his castle walls planning his next attack. Again and again, Shingen had squared off against Kenshin on the plains of Kawanakajima, but he'd never managed to demolish the other leader's armies. Maybe this summer. Maybe this would be the battle …

Shingen's wife touched his arm, drawing his thoughts back to the ceremony. His nephew was presenting a new kimono to Chiyome. The wedding was over. Thankfully. Shingen had a battle to plan.

A village, summer 1561

THIRTEEN-YEAR-OLD AKI, thin and barefoot, hovered in the doorway of her thatched-roof hut. She stared up at the samurai warriors, their armor marked with Takeda Shingen's personal crest. As the sun rose behind them, they seemed to glow. It was as if otherworldly creatures had appeared on the dirt road through her village. One of them wore a bow across his back. The carved wooden arc was twice Aki's height.

When the soldiers called out, farmers and their wives emerged from the huts to either side. Aki's mother was sick with fever and couldn't leave her bed. Only Aki's father stepped outside.

She wanted to leap for his ankles and hold him back. But that would have shamed him.

19

"What's happening?" her mother whispered from the mattress behind her.

Aki didn't answer. How could she explain that the soldiers were taking him away? Somehow, with little armor and borrowed weapons, he'd be expected to fight for his daimyo at a place called Kawanakajima, a place none of them had ever seen.

Her mother drifted from consciousness again. Aki almost wished she could do the same.

"When will they come back?" Aki asked her neighbor, a woman whose husband had also marched away.

Her neighbor didn't know.

Aki made herself a breakfast of porridge, but she let the fire grow too hot and the millet pot charred. The burnt taste didn't leave her mouth all day, not even when she went to the temple.

"When will the men come back from the war?" she asked the monk.

"Pray for them," he said.

When she went home, her mother's skin burned hotter than before. Aki wondered how many prayers the ancestors could hear in a single day.

CHIYOME SAID A SILENT PRAYER as she helped her husband adjust the straps that held his red lacquer chestplate in place. Even with his iron helmet still held loosely in his hands, Moritoki seemed huge in his armor.

"I married a giant," she teased.

He smiled back at her, but Chiyome could tell his mind was already far away, on the coming clashes. This would be the fourth time the army marched to the plains of Kawanakajima, and Shingen was sending more men than ever before.

"Be careful," Chiyome whispered.

"Always," he said. He leaned down to wrap his arms around her one last time, while they were still alone.

A few months ago, she'd married a stranger. But during their first spring together, she'd slowly started to understand him. He was as proud and ambitious as she was. (Like her mother had said, a good match!) He was strong, like all the samurai, but capable of kindness, too.

After their goodbyes, Moritoki left the house, donned his helmet, and strode away to take his place at the head of his troops.

Chiyome watched with mixed feelings. She'd miss him, she realized. But more than that, she hated to be left behind. Her dreams of becoming a ninja—taking her own place in the battle—hadn't faded.

Kawanakajima,
September 1561

FROM THE WEST BANK OF THE RIVER, Takeda Shingen could see the entire plains. His samurai formed battle lines below, their family pennants flapping in the wind, as the army of Uesugi Kenshin marched steadily closer.

Shingen scowled. He'd sent a secret force to overtake the enemy during the night, but Kenshin had guessed his plans and launched a counterattack. Now, as Shingen watched, unit after unit of samurai crashed against his troops. The grasslands rang with whizzing arrows, screaming horses, and clashing swords.

One by one, Shingen's generals fell. Then Kenshin himself broke
through the lines and charged the famous daimyo. Armed with only
the iron fan he used to signal his troops, Shingen desperately defended
himself. Finally, one of his guards managed to spear Kenshin's horse.

The enemy leader fled.

The samurai still collided below, but Shingen spotted hope. His
secret force, the one sent out in the night, had returned. They sped along
the riverbank and slashed their way through the flank of Kenshin's army.

Soon, the enemy was forced to retreat. They'd lost almost
three-quarters of their men. But Shingen's army was battered as well,
and many of his best commanders and soldiers lay dead—including his
nephew, Moritoki.

CHIYOME CROSSED THE COURTYARD of Takeda Shingen's manor house.

"Hurry up," she ordered a servant girl dawdling by the woodpile.

This was her role since the army had marched away at the beginning of the summer. She supervised the workers, ordered the dinners, and watched over the family finances.

She'd never been so bored in her life.

The echo of hooves caught her attention. A moment later, a lone messenger entered the gates, and the guards ushered him toward her.

He bowed low and began to speak as Chiyome listened in shock.

The daimyo's nephew ...

a fierce battle ...

an honorable death.

The other women of the household hurried to Chiyome's side, ushered her into the house, and poured her tea. Perhaps they expected her to cry, but she stared blankly at the wall. She'd barely started to know Moritoki, and now he was gone.

Without a husband, what would happen to her? She couldn't go home. She was part of Takeda Shingen's family now. And as a widow, her options would be limited. She could stay in the manor house and take care of other women's children. Or she could leave and join a religious retreat. Either way, the rest of her life would be quiet, simple, and alone.

Then she did cry.

The women were quick to gather around and comfort her, but they didn't understand. Not really.

CHIYOME PAUSED IN FRONT OF TAKEDA SHINGEN'S DOOR. The army had finally returned, smaller after the summer's losses, and she had immediately requested an audience with the daimyo. She'd made her decision. Now she had to convince him of her plan.

Be patient. Conquer fear.

Even as she trembled inside, she held her head high.

She entered the room, bowed to Shingen, and exchanged a few words of greeting with him. Then she took a deep breath.

"I've heard that the other daimyos are so scared of spies, they surround themselves only with sons and nephews, or trusted childhood friends," she said.

Shingen grunted in agreement.

"I've even heard the story of a failed assassination," she said. "A ninja crept into the bedchamber before dawn and stabbed the enemy daimyo where he slept … except the daimyo rose early to pray each morning, and so escaped his own death. The ninja stabbed only the mattress."

Shingen was watching her keenly now. Abruptly, he waved an arm, and the servants surrounding them backed from the room. Chiyome knew why. The failed assassination attempt had been ordered by Shingen himself.

He narrowed his eyes and leaned toward her. "Why do we discuss this?"

Be patient. Conquer fear.

But even as she repeated the mantra in her head, the words burst from her. "A woman never would have made that mistake, Daimyo. *I* never would have made that mistake. I would have learned the man's habits before I attacked."

Shingen's laugh was like thunder, shaking the paper screens and causing one of the servants to peek cautiously through the doorway. Shingen waved the man away again.

"Perhaps women could succeed where men have failed," she suggested.

Shingen nodded, still smiling. "What do you have in mind?" he said.

She had no shortage of ideas. All those days in the manor house had given her plenty of time to plan.

RAIN DRIPPED THROUGH THE THATCHED roof, and Aki shivered as she cleared tables. It was late. Only a few men lingered over cups of sake. She wished they would all go home so she could curl up in her corner of the storeroom and sleep.

As she turned, her hands full of dishes, a small man at a nearby table grabbed her arm.

Aki froze. Drunk men could be dangerous, and the tavern owner would do nothing to protect her. She was an orphan now, and easily replaced.

"Do you read?" the man said.

Aki realized it wasn't a man at all. It was a woman wrapped in a long cape made of woven hemp palm, with a wide-brimmed hat pulled low over her eyes.

Aki nodded. She'd learned to read at the temple, before her father was killed in the battles and before the daimyo had seized their farm.

The woman loosened her grasp on Aki's arm.

"Do you like your work here?" she asked.

Aki hesitated. The owner was probably nearby, and the wrong answer would get her a cane mark across her shoulders.

Her thoughts must have shown in her face. The woman chuckled.

"Find me your boss," she said. "Tell him I have an offer he can't refuse."

C HIYOME STARED DOWN AT THE FIVE YOUNG WOMEN kneeling on the woven mats. They were the first students to gather in this old wooden building she'd chosen as her school.

"A charity school, to train orphans as shrine maidens," she'd told the neighbors, who had smiled at her approvingly.

Over the last few weeks, she'd traveled to villages ravaged by war. She'd searched each one for orphans—the daughters of farmers who'd been killed in battle.

It wasn't easy to find girls who fit her needs. Most of the village girls were illiterate, and scared of their shadows. And many were pock-marked by disease. Chiyome needed girls who could tempt samurai to tell their secrets.

But now, as she stood in her school and looked at the smooth, pretty faces before her, she knew she had chosen her students well. She let her eyes rest on Aki, her first recruit.

Chiyome cleared her throat and began.

"You were told this was a religious school. That isn't true," she said.

Aki glanced up.

"You will learn the skills of *miko*, Shinto shrine maidens," Chiyome said, "but only because those skills will allow you to travel. You will travel from shrine to shrine, praying to the spirits and the ancestors and learning more about your religion. But while traveling, you will listen for the secrets of daimyos. You will count their samurai and memorize their roads. You will report back to me."

Aki was staring. Chiyome glared until the girl dropped her gaze.

"You will be shinobi," Chiyome said.

Shinobi. Ninjas. There was a rustling through the row.

She told them more. Their daimyo wanted ninjas for his own secret army, she explained. Ninjas made great bodyguards and perfect spies. While proud samurai warriors clashed on the battlefields, ninjas slipped into enemy lands, counted troops, mapped roads, and listened for battle strategies. They worked as undercover agents, and even assassins.

"Your lessons begin now," she said.

Outskirts of Nazu, 1563

CHIYOME STOOD AT THE EDGE of the bamboo forest beside the falls, watching icy water pour over Aki. The girl sat completely still below the deluge. She didn't even look like she was shivering.

She's ready, Chiyome thought.

In the past months Chiyome had trained her first batch of students in every skill imaginable. They'd learned *hensōjutsu*: how to observe the mannerisms of others and impersonate all sorts of people—shrine maidens, servants, or entertainers. Every one of these orphaned farm girls could pour tea for a samurai as if she'd been born to an upper-class family.

They'd studied self-defense, first aid, and outdoor survival. How to hide on a dark night, and how to change disguises so they weren't seen when the moon was bright. How to conceal sharpened metal claws in their belts, and slip them onto their fingers when needed. How to boil wild plants to make medicines. How to use rice wine as invisible ink, and send torch signals through the night.

Today marked Aki's final challenge. After this, she would travel east, crossing the border between the lands of Shingen and those of his enemy, Uesugi Kenshin.

At Chiyome's gesture, Aki unfolded herself and walked carefully over the rocks toward her, moving faster as she gained confidence.

Then Aki slipped. One of the stones rolled beneath her feet, splashing into the stream.

"Be patient," Chiyome said sternly.

But she smiled to herself as she passed on the wisdom of her own instructor. Her old sensei had been right. Patience had brought Chiyome everything she'd dreamed of. Her first group of recruits would be heading out on their missions, and new orphans were arriving every month. Soon she'd have ninjas working across the region. She'd know every secret in Japan. She'd be the most valuable weapon in Shingen's army, though no one would ever know.

A border outpost,
one month later

THE GUARDS STEPPED FORWARD TO BLOCK THE GIRL approaching the checkpoint. Not many people were allowed to pass between the territories of Takeda Shingen and those of Uesugi Kenshin.

But the guards scanned her red and white outfit: clearly, she was a traveling shrine maiden. When one guard asked about his ancestors, she promised to pray to them.

They ushered her through. A shrine maiden was no threat to anyone.

The next day, the shrine maiden stepped off the road and into the edge of the thick forest as a battalion of samurai passed. There were so many soldiers, the ground vibrated. She reached into her pocket and scooped a small handful of stones. For every ten men who marched by her, she dropped a stone.

No one thought twice about the girl waiting along the roadside, playing with pebbles.

They should have paid closer attention. Once the soldiers had passed, Aki adjusted her robes and shook the rest of the stones from her pocket into her palm. She'd counted them that morning, so by tallying those that remained, she knew how many soldiers had passed. She'd encode the information in a letter and send it to Chiyome.

But first, Aki had other missions to accomplish. Keeping to the edge of the forest and spending her nights in the woods, she made her way undetected toward Kasugayama Castle, until the walls were finally in sight.

Glancing around to make sure no one was watching, Aki pulled off her shrine maiden garments and changed into a simple robe. She pulled a wide-brimmed hat low over her forehead. Then she gathered an armful of wood and began the steep climb past rice paddies, temples, and stables. As she approached the gates, she slid behind a group of gossiping servants, easily blending with them. Within moments, she was inside the walls.

While she tended various fires, Aki paced the courtyard and counted the storerooms. She noted the size of the family's multi-tiered house, and the positions of the samurai barracks. Slipping back through the gate, she hurried downhill toward the cover of the forest.

Thump thump thump. She heard footsteps behind her. She stopped herself from looking back, not wanting to raise suspicion. As she left the road, her hand slipped into her wide belt to pull out what looked like large seeds. Casually, she scattered a few behind her. If someone were following her, those seed-pods—actually spiky pieces of metal called caltrops—would pierce his straw sandals, stopping him in his tracks.

The footsteps faded into the distance. False alarm.

Tomorrow, Aki would pass her information to another of Chiyome's traveling girls. Then she'd go back to work. She'd find a job as a kitchen maid, or befriend a samurai. Who knew what secrets she might learn?

She smiled to herself as darkness fell. People said that ninjas could walk on water, pass through walls, and fly. Aki couldn't do any of those things. But today, she'd felt almost invisible.

Army camp,
Mikawa province, 1572

T AKEDA SHINGEN SLID FROM HIS HORSE and staggered into his tent. He lowered his bulk onto one of the mats. While he struggled to catch his breath, his mind began to wander.

For more than thirty years, he had battled for land and power, trying to unite more and more regions under his rule. He'd conquered many of the lesser daimyos. He'd even managed—barely—to hold back the powerful Tokugawa Ieyasu, a daimyo who'd embraced the use of the new muskets and cannons.

Shingen's territories had once been landlocked, but over the years he'd fought his way to the Pacific coast and now there was even a navy under his command. He'd always been a master of strategy, adopting spears for his cavalry and muskets for his foot soldiers. Learning more about his enemies than they would ever guess.

But now, Shingen was exhausted. Wounds from previous battles flared. Most nights, he woke up clawing for breath.

He was supposed to be launching another assault against Ieyasu. And he knew no one else could lead the battle. His son was still young and reckless. But there was no way Shingen could lead, either. While his samurai waited for orders, the great daimyo lay in his tent, unable to rise.

As night fell, a robed form slipped through the entranceway. An assassin? Shingen struggled to pull himself upright, and failed.

It was a woman. She knelt beside his mattress and bowed her head.

"So it's true," she said.

"Chiyome. Do you have news for me?" It had been a good decision, ten years ago now, to let her open her school. She'd brought him secrets from all corners of the country. And more than one of Shingen's rivals had met a mysterious death at the hands of her students …

But today, Chiyome shook her head. "It's too late for news," she said.

He could feel it was true. He was passing on to a new life, a new destiny. And the country itself was changing.

Nazu, a week later

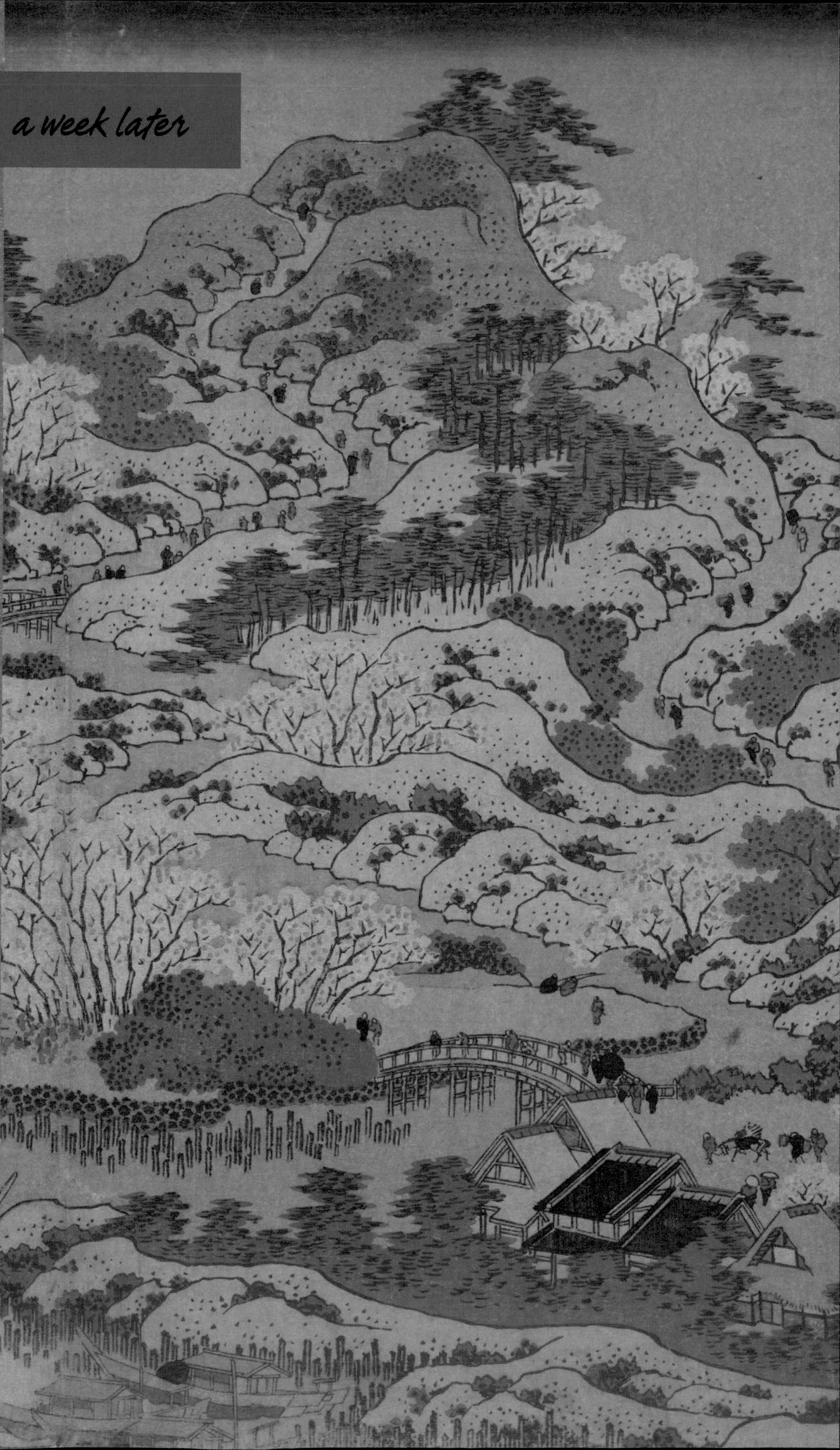

CHIYOME PACKED A SMALL BAG. Shingen had died a few days before and she'd returned to the school right away, refusing to stay and take orders from his hotheaded son. She wasn't going to wait here for enemy assassins, either.

She'd sent word to her ninjas—over two hundred of them now, spread between enemy castles and distant towns. They'd have to find new masters or new occupations. The world was changing, anyway— Tokugawa Ieyasu was making alliances and uniting territories. People were tired of constant war. Perhaps Japan would not need ninjas for much longer.

Chiyome glanced one more time around her school. She felt proud of what she'd accomplished. Through her network of spies, she'd become one of the most powerful people in the region, and passed her skills to others. She knew every secret in Japan. She had money, now, and options. She was still a strong woman. She could return home to her village in Kōga. Or she could approach one of the rising daimyos and offer her services. Ieyasu might not need spies and assassins, but he'd still want bodyguards and security officers.

Wrapped once more in a hemp-palm cape, with only her straw sandals and a small bag of supplies, Chiyome stepped onto the road.

There was no telling where she might go.

Fact and Fiction

Some of the characters in this story are real, and some are invented.

Takeda Shingen was a powerful daimyo who seized control of his father's land in 1540 and proceeded to expand his territory through a series of wars.

Mochizuki Moritoki was a real samurai, the nephew of Takeda Shingen. He died in 1561 in a battle against Uesugi Kenshin.

Mochizuki Chiyome was *probably* real. In the 1600s, Japanese writers and artists created storybooks, the ancestors of today's graphic novels. Some of these tales featured a woman ninja trainer, a widow who lost her husband and went to work for his uncle, training spies in an undercover school. There are enough of these stories, and enough details that match, to make historians believe Chiyome was a real person.

If Chiyome was real, then so were her spy girls. But we have no written record of them. The character of Aki is imaginary.

Takeda Shingen died in 1573, possibly of pneumonia. By then, the world was beginning to change. Over the next decades, a few warlords seized more power than ever before. Small states began to merge. In 1600, a daimyo named Tokugawa Ieyasu won a decisive victory. By 1603, he'd united all of Japan.

Free from the constant fighting and feuding, Japanese people began rebuilding their towns and cities. They had time to explore painting and literature, to build architectural wonders and design fabulous gardens. It was the dawn of a time known as Japan's Great Peace, which would last more than 250 years.

That's when storybooks began to feature Chiyome's story. And her tale has survived for centuries. Even today, she appears as a character in video games and comic books, historical novels and action films. In some, she's a cute half-cat. In others, she's a dangerous martial artist.

People remember and glamorize Chiyome in part because she was such a unique character—a female fighter in a male-dominated world, and a teacher of deadly, secret skills. But her story also survives because she lived at such an interesting time—a world of war, on the brink of a Great Peace to come.

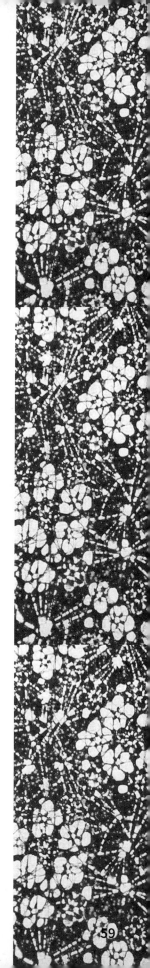

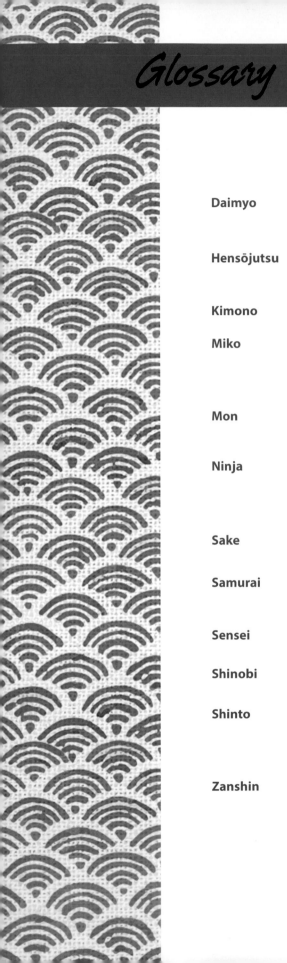

Glossary

Daimyo A local lord in Japan. In the 1500s, there were hundreds of these warlords, each with his own land, castle, and army of samurai warriors.

Hensōjutsu The ninja practice of observing mannerisms and details, in order to better disguise oneself or impersonate others.

Kimono A wide-sleeved robe historically worn by both men and women.

Miko Shrine maidens who traveled between Shinto shrines, tending the sites and learning more about the religion. They were believed to communicate with spirits and the ghosts of ancestors.

Mon A round metal crest used to identify families or clans. The mon most often used by the Takeda clan was a pattern of four diamonds.

Ninja A type of undercover soldier with skills passed down through families and clans. Some daimyos openly hired ninjas as bodyguards, then used others as hidden spies and assassins.

Sake A wine made from fermented rice.

Samurai A highly trained warrior, armed with swords or bows, and later with firearms.

Sensei A Japanese word for "teacher."

Shinobi Another name for ninja.

Shinto One of Japan's most ancient religions. Followers worship the spirits of nature and of their ancestors. Over the centuries, Shinto incorporated some of the teachings of Buddhism.

Zanshin A mental state of calm awareness practiced by ninjas.

Further Reading

Glaser, Jason, and Don Roley. *Ninja*. Mankato: Capstone Press, 2007.

Hartz, Paula. *Shinto*. New York: Facts on File, 2004.

Malam, John. *100 Things You Should Know About Samurai*. Broomall: Mason Crest Publishers, 2010.

Ollhoff, Jim. *Ninja*. Edina: ABDO Publishing, 2008.

Park, Louise. *The Japanese Samurai*. New York: Marshall Cavendish Benchmark, 2010.

Turnbull, Stephen. *Real Ninja*. New York: Enchanted Lion Books, 2008.

Turnbull, Stephen. *Samurai Women 1184–1877*. Oxford: Osprey Publishing, 2010.

Yoda, Hiroko, and Matt Alt. *Ninja Attack!* Tokyo: Kodansha International, 2010.

Selected Sources

Bertrand, John. "Techniques that made ninjas feared in 15th-century Japan still set the standard for covert ops." *Military History*, March 2006, 12–19.

Bincsik, Monika. "Japanese Weddings in the Edo Period (1615-1868)." From the website of The Metropolitan Museum of Art. metmuseum.org/toah/hd/jwed/hd_jwed.htm.

Cummins, Antony. *In Search of the Ninja*. Gloucestershire: The History Press, 2012.

Cummins, Antony. *Samurai and Ninja*. Tokyo: Tuttle Publishing, 2015.

Cummins, Antony, and Yoshie Minami. *The Book of Ninja: The Bansenshukai*. London: Watkins Publishing, 2013.

Cummins, Antony, and Yoshie Minami. *Samurai War Stories*. Gloucestershire: The History Press, 2013.

Cummins, Antony, and Yoshie Minami. *True Path of the Ninja: The Definitive Translation of the* Shoninki. Tokyo: Tuttle Publishing, 2011.

Goto, Michiko. "The Lives and Roles of Women of Various Classes in the *Ie* of Late Medieval Japan." *International Journal of Asian Studies*, July 2006, 183–210.

Hsia, Hsiao-Chuan, and John H. Scanzoni. "Rethinking the Roles of Japanese Women." *Journal of Comparative Family Studies*, Summer 1996, 309–29.

Kurushima, Noriko. "Marriage and Female Inheritance in Medieval Japan." *International Journal of Asian Studies*, June 2004, 223–45.

Man, John. *Ninja*. New York: HarperCollins Publishers, 2012.

Turnbull, Stephen. *Samurai*. Oxford: Osprey Publishing, 2003.

Turnbull, Stephen. *Samurai Women 1184–1877*. Oxford: Osprey Publishing, 2010.

About the Author and Illustrator

Tanya Lloyd Kyi loves to meld stories of history, pop culture, and science. Her nonfiction books for young readers include *Eyes and Spies*, *Extreme Battlefields*, *DNA Detective*, and *When the Worst Happens*. Tanya has also written several novels for teens, including *Prince of Pot* and *Anywhere but Here*. She lives in Vancouver, British Columbia, with her husband and two children.

Celia Krampien grew up in a house in the woods on the Bruce Peninsula in Ontario, Canada, and spent her childhood reading, observing the local wildlife, and climbing trees. She currently lives in Oakville, Ontario, with her partner, and enjoys working alongside her silly cat and going for long walks with her nosy beagle. Celia's illustrations have appeared in publications including *The Globe and Mail*, *Scientific American*, and *The Los Angeles Times*.

Image credits

Cover *Landscapes of the Four Seasons* by Sesshū Tōyō; **2–3** map taken from *A History of Japan* by James Murdoch and Isoh Yamagata, 1903; **4** *Landscape* by Sesshū Tōyō/Wikimedia Commons; **9** *Bo Ya Plays the Qin as Zhong Ziqi Listens* by Circle of Kano Motonobu/ Mary Griggs Burke Collection, Gift of the Mary and Jackson Burke Foundation, 2015/The Met; **12** *Zhou Maoshu Appreciating Lotuses* by Kanō Masanobu/Wikimedia Commons; **14** *Cottage by a Mountain Stream* by Kichizan Minchō; **16** *Illustrated Tale of the Heiji Civil War*, Wikimedia Commons; **18** *View of Ama-no-Hashidate* by Sesshū Tōyō/Wikimedia Commons; **23** *Landscape with a Solitary Traveler* by Yosa Buson/Wikimedia Commons; **26** *A Retired Official's Homecoming* by Watanabe Gentai/Wikimedia Commons; **29** *Two women gathering lotus blossoms*/Library of Congress Prints and Photographs Division, LC-DIG-jpd-02136; **30** *Lake Pavillion Spring View* by Sesshū Tōyō (attrib.)/Wikimedia Commons; **34** *Evening Rain at Karasaki Pine Tree* by Utagawa Hiroshige/ Rogers Fund, 1919/The Met; **39** *Autumn and Winter Landscape* by Sesshū Tōyō/Wikimedia Commons; **40** *Landscape with Waterfall* by Nakabayashi Chikutō/ The Harry G. C. Packard Collection of Asian Art/The Met; **42** *Narihira's Journey to the East* by Maruyama Ōkyo/Wikimedia Commons; **44** *Lofty Mt. Lu* by Shen Zhou/Wikimedia Commons; **50** *Landscapes of the Four Seasons* by Keison/ Mary Griggs Burke Collection, Gift of the Mary and Jackson Burke Foundation, 2015/The Met; **54** *Mount Tempo at Setchu from the Mouth of the River Aji* by Hokusai Katsushika/Library of Congress Prints and Photographs Division, LC-DIG-jpd-00821; **58** *View of Sanshui* by Suzuki Gako/Wikimedia Commons